Cool School

Written by John Parker
Illustrated by Fraser Williamson

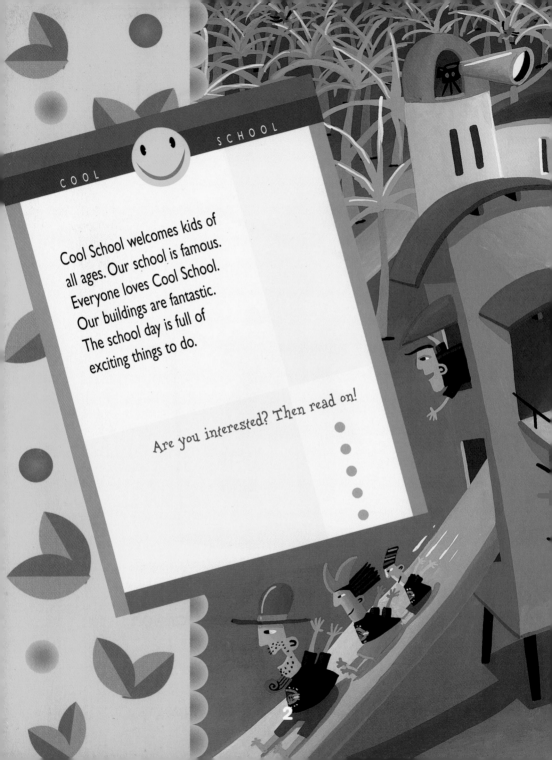

Cool School welcomes kids of all ages. Our school is famous. Everyone loves Cool School. Our buildings are fantastic. The school day is full of exciting things to do.

Are you interested? Then read on!

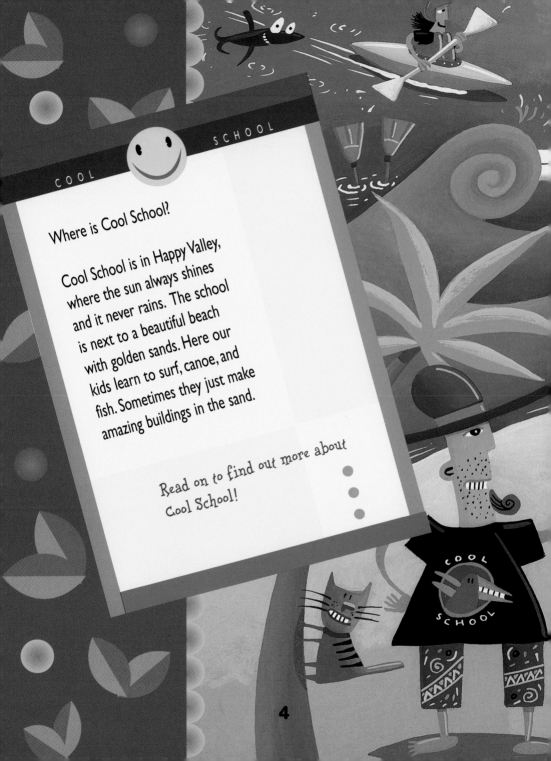

Where is Cool School?

Cool School is in Happy Valley, where the sun always shines and it never rains. The school is next to a beautiful beach with golden sands. Here our kids learn to surf, canoe, and fish. Sometimes they just make amazing buildings in the sand.

Read on to find out more about Cool School!

COOL SCHOOL

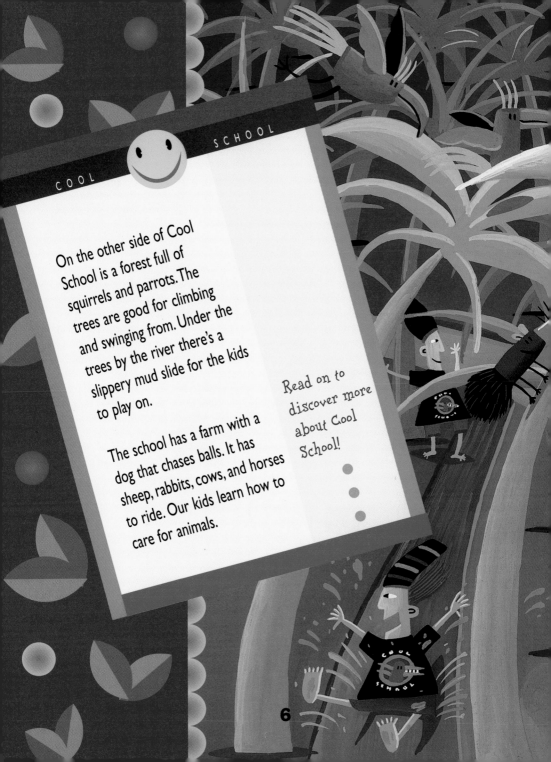

On the other side of Cool School is a forest full of squirrels and parrots. The trees are good for climbing and swinging from. Under the trees by the river there's a slippery mud slide for the kids to play on.

The school has a farm with a dog that chases balls. It has sheep, rabbits, cows, and horses to ride. Our kids learn how to care for animals.

Read on to discover more about Cool School!

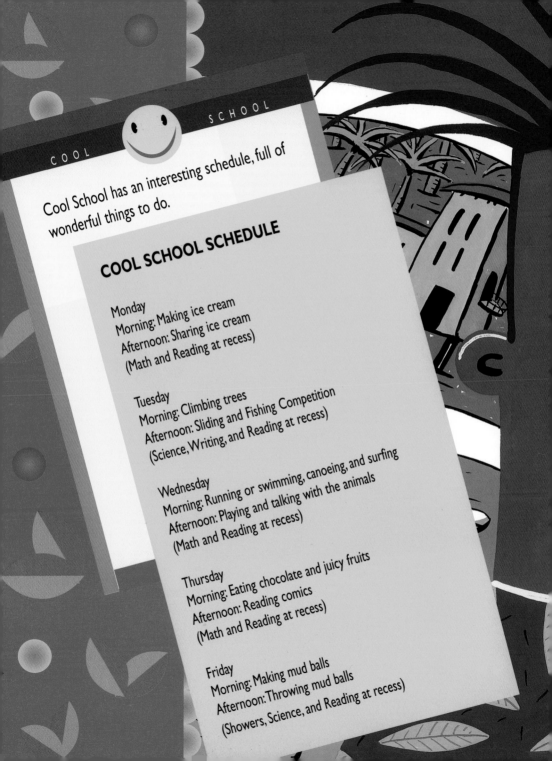

COOL · SCHOOL

Cool School has an interesting schedule, full of wonderful things to do.

COOL SCHOOL SCHEDULE

Monday
Morning: Making ice cream
Afternoon: Sharing ice cream
(Math and Reading at recess)

Tuesday
Morning: Climbing trees
Afternoon: Sliding and Fishing Competition
(Science, Writing, and Reading at recess)

Wednesday
Morning: Running or swimming, canoeing, and surfing
Afternoon: Playing and talking with the animals
(Math and Reading at recess)

Thursday
Morning: Eating chocolate and juicy fruits
Afternoon: Reading comics
(Math and Reading at recess)

Friday
Morning: Making mud balls
Afternoon: Throwing mud balls
(Showers, Science, and Reading at recess)

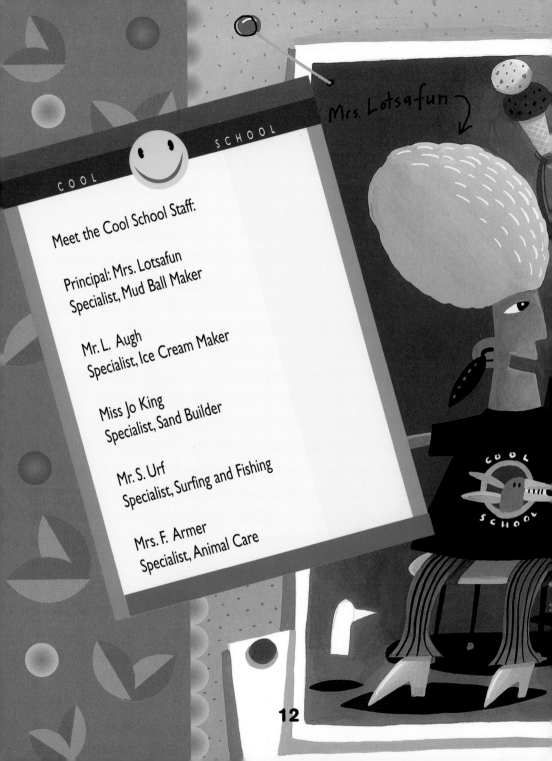

Mrs. Lotsafun

COOL SCHOOL

Meet the Cool School Staff:

Principal: Mrs. Lotsafun
Specialist, Mud Ball Maker

Mr. L. Augh
Specialist, Ice Cream Maker

Miss Jo King
Specialist, Sand Builder

Mr. S. Urf
Specialist, Surfing and Fishing

Mrs. F. Armer
Specialist, Animal Care

12

How much does Cool School cost?

Cool School is completely free.
All children are welcome.
All you need when you come to
Cool School is a friendly face.

Does Cool School sound like the
school for you?

Phone 1-800-555-8287
E-mail: coolschool@eliktric.com

Brochures

Brochures persuade people to come and see something, like a school. They describe the place and the things that happen there.

How to write a brochure:

Step One
Introduce the place.

Cool School welcomes kids of all ages. Our school is famous. Everyone loves Cool School. Our buildings are fantastic. The school day is full of exciting things to do.

Step Two
Describe where it is.

Where is Cool School?

Cool School is in Happy Valley, where the sun always shines and it never rains. The school is next to a beautiful beach with golden sands. Here, our kids learn to surf, canoe, and fish. Sometimes they just make amazing buildings in the sand.

Step Three
Describe the things that happen there.

COOL SCHOOL SCHEDULE

Monday
Morning: Making ice cream
Afternoon: Sharing ice cream
(Math and Reading at recess)

Tuesday
Morning: Climbing trees
Afternoon: Sliding and Fishing Competition
(Science, Writing, and Reading at recess)

Wednesday
Morning: Running or swimming, canoeing, and surfing
Afternoon: Playing and talking with the animals
(Math and Reading at recess)

Thursday
Morning: Eating chocolate and juicy fruits
Afternoon: Reading comics
(Math and Reading at recess)

...day
...ning: Making mud balls
...noon: Throwing mud balls
...rs, Science, and Reading at recess)

Step Four
Give details about who can enroll, and how.

Cool School is completely free.
All children are welcome.
All you need when you come to
Cool School is a friendly face.

Does Cool School sound like the
school for you?

Phone 1-800-555-8287
E-mail: coolschool@eliktric.com

Guide Notes

Title: Cool School
Stage: Fluency (2)

Text Form: Brochure
Approach: Guided Reading
Processes: Thinking Critically, Exploring Language, Processing Information
Written and Visual Focus: Brochure

THINKING CRITICALLY
(sample questions)
- Why do you think Cool School is famous?
- Look at the school schedule. Which day would you enjoy the most? Why?
- Why do you think the kids say they wish they could stay at Cool School forever?
- Why do you think you need a friendly face to go to Cool School?

EXPLORING LANGUAGE

Terminology
Spread, author and illustrator credits, ISBN number

Vocabulary
Clarify: surf, fantastic, specialist, e-mail, completely
Nouns: school, sun, canoe, buildings, trees
Verbs: surf, fish, climb, swim
Singular/plural: kid/kids, school/schools, parrot/parrots, animal/animals

Print Conventions
Parenthesis: (Math and Reading at recess)
Colon, apostrophe – contraction (there's)
Abbreviation: Mr. L., e-mail (electronic mail)

Phonological Patterns
Focus on short and long vowel **i** (k**i**ds, sw**i**nging, th**i**ngs, exc**i**ting, sl**i**de, r**i**de)
Discuss root words – amazing, exciting, writing, sliding, making, beautiful, running
Look at suffix **ist** (special**ist**), **y** (juic**y**), **ly** (complete**ly**, friend**ly**), **ful** (wonder**ful**)